This book belongs to:

Owl's World

Disney's Out & About With Pooh
A Grow and Learn Library

Published by Advance Publishers
© 1996 Disney Enterprises, Inc.
Based on the Pooh stories by A. A. Milne © The Pooh Properties Trust.

Written by Ronald Kidd
Illustrated by Arkadia Illustration Ltd.
Designed by Vickey Bolling
Produced by Bumpy Slide Books

ISBN:1-885222-72-6
10 9 8 7 6

Most of the time Piglet tried to be a very brave animal. He did well in the mornings, and afternoons were an especially good time. It was just nights that bothered him.

One night Piglet was lying in bed, trying to fall asleep, when he heard a sound. He dived beneath the covers, sure that he was surrounded by monsters.

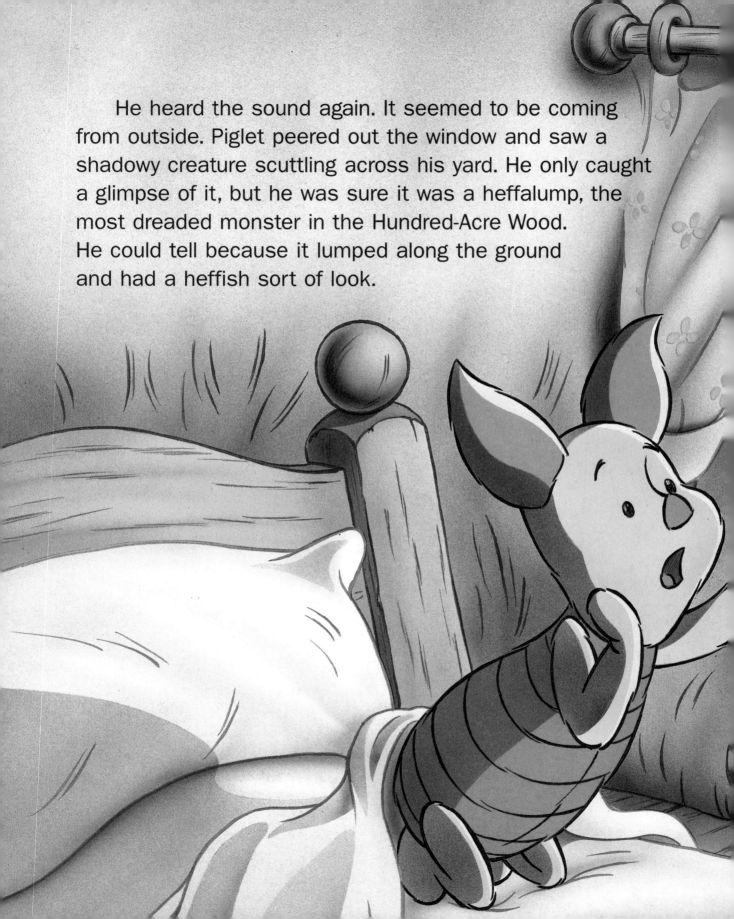

He heard the sound again. It seemed to be coming from outside. Piglet peered out the window and saw a shadowy creature scuttling across his yard. He only caught a glimpse of it, but he was sure it was a heffalump, the most dreaded monster in the Hundred-Acre Wood. He could tell because it lumped along the ground and had a heffish sort of look.

Piglet went back to bed, but he was too frightened
to sleep. So he went to see his friend Winnie the Pooh.

"Pooh, what are we going to do?" asked Piglet, wringing his tiny hands.

Pooh paced back and forth, saying, "Think, think, think." Finally he stopped and said, "We could have some honey."

A short time later, the honey jar was empty and Pooh was full. He looked up and said in a sticky sort of voice, "Piglet, I don't know much about creatures who go bump in the night. But I think I know someone who might."

And so they went to see Owl, who was perched outside his house, reading a book.

"Ah, there you are," said Owl, as if Pooh and Piglet always came to see him in the middle of the night. "I was just reading about owl inventors. Did I ever tell you — "

"Pardon me, Owl," said Pooh, "but I was just wondering if you have another kind of book — on things that make noises in the night, such as heffalumps."

Owl gazed kindly at Piglet. "The best way to learn about the night isn't from books," he said. "It's by going out and seeing for yourself. Would you like to do that?"

Piglet shivered. "C-c-c-ould we wait until tomorrow morning?"

But Owl had already flown off his perch and was setting off down the path. "Come along, now," he said.

Pooh and Piglet looked at each other, then joined hands and followed Owl into the forest.

As they passed beneath a tree, Piglet noticed tiny lights flickering on and off in the sky. "What are those?" he asked.

"Fireflies," said Owl. "They're a type of flying beetle. They light up to send each other messages."

While the three friends watched, the fireflies swirled ahead of them, lighting their way.

"Some animals, such as Piglets and Pooh bears, go to sleep when it gets dark," Owl continued. "But other animals rest during the day and come out at night. You may not always see them, but you can often hear them. For instance, do you hear that sound?"

"Pardon me," said Pooh, patting his tummy.

Owl smiled. "I didn't mean your tummy noise, Pooh," he said. "I was talking about that chirping sound. It's made by crickets."

"Crickets talk a lot, don't they?" said Piglet.

"Oh, they don't make that sound with their mouths," Owl explained. "They make it by rubbing their wings together. The hotter it is, the faster they rub and the more they chirp."

Pooh tilted his head to one side and said, "Now I hear a croaking sound."

"I know that one," said Piglet. "It's a frog. Sometimes frogs come out in the daytime, too."

Owl said, "Frogs especially enjoy nighttime because it's cool, and their skin stays nice and wet — just the way they like it."

Suddenly there was a noise behind them, and Piglet whirled around. "There it is!" he cried. "The heffalump!"

Owl and Pooh turned to look, but the heffalump was gone.
"I saw it, really," Piglet told them breathlessly. "It was right
there, lumping across the path."

"Oh, bother," said Pooh, "I just remembered something I need to do at home."

"What is it?" Piglet asked.

Pooh said, "Hide under the bed."

"You can go home if you'd like," said Owl. "But the more

you learn about things, the less frightening they are. It's even true of heffalumps."

"Then let's keep going," Piglet said in a small but very brave voice.

Owl led them through the forest, saying, "Not all nighttime animals make loud noises. Sometimes the only sound you hear is a soft rustling of leaves. It could be a mouse, a fox, a deer, or some other animal."

"I hear a little buzzing sound," said Pooh, swatting his neck.

Owl said, "That's a mosquito. They come out at night, along with lots of other insects."

Owl bent down and showed them a bunch of white flowers. "Animals aren't the only things that come out in the dark," he said. "Some plants only bloom at night, like these honeysuckle blossoms."

"There's a butterfly on one of them," said Piglet.

Owl said, "That's not a butterfly; it's a moth. Moths fly at night because they like the sweet smell the night-blooming flowers make."

There was another noise behind them. This time all three friends whirled around, hoping to catch sight of the heffalump. Sure enough, there it was, standing in the middle of the path.

"See? A heffalump!" cried Piglet. "I told you."
Pooh would have answered, but he was busy hiding behind Piglet, who was hiding behind Owl.

Pooh and Piglet thought Owl must be scared, too.
Instead, Owl started to chuckle.

"I'm sorry to disappoint you, Piglet," he said, "but your
heffalump isn't really a heffalump at all. It's an opossum,

and it's probably more frightened than you are. An opposum is another kind of animal that comes out at night."

"Oh, no!" said Pooh, looking at the motionless creature. "I think we've scared it to death."

Owl rolled the opossum over, then picked it up by its tail. The opossum still didn't move. Owl explained, "It's not really dead. It's just pretending. That's the opossum's way of protecting itself, so that other animals won't bother it."

"The opossum is strange-looking," Owl went on, "but it's really quite interesting. It has a pouch for carrying its babies, just like Kanga. It has thumbs almost like the ones

that people have, and it uses its tail like a washcloth. Not only that, it eats almost anything!"

As he set the opossum back down, the first rays of sunlight came peeking through the branches. Owl yawned. "I'm getting sleepy," he said. "I think I'll go home and take a nap."

"Me, too," piped Piglet.

Pooh brightened. "Time for breakfast. Maybe I'll have a little smackerel of something."

It had been a busy evening. Piglet and Pooh had learned about the nighttime, and they had met lots of new animals — fireflies, crickets, frogs, mosquitoes, moths, and even an opossum.

Piglet smiled. The next time he met a heffalump, he might just decide to be brave and say "How do you do?" After all, a heffalump might be another interesting creature of the night.